PIGGINS

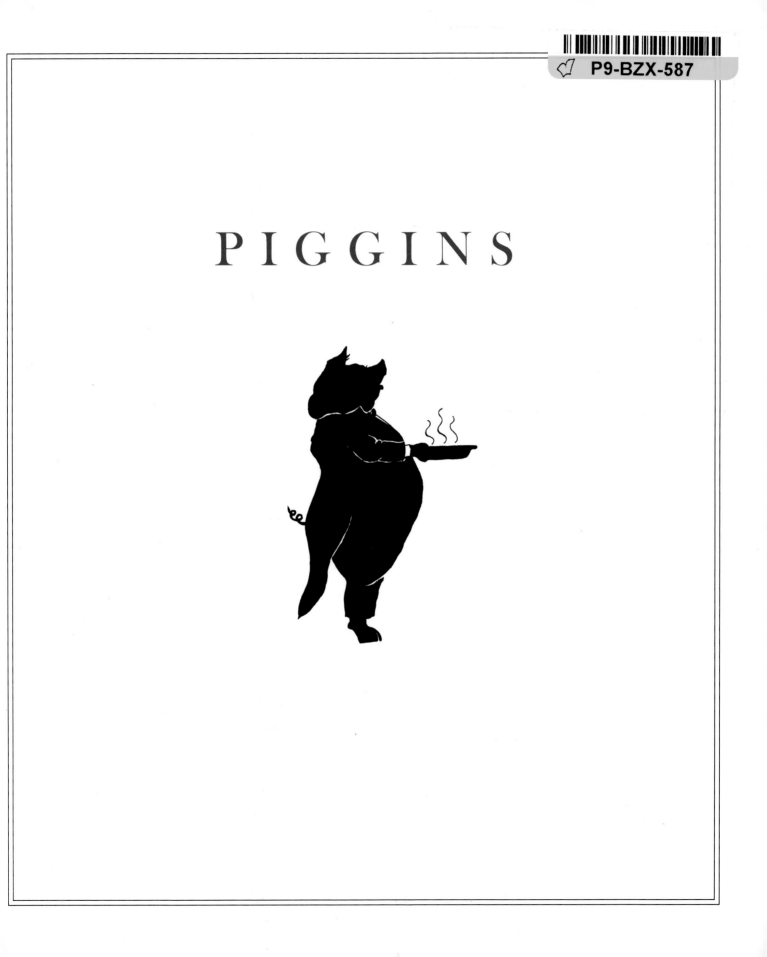

PIGGINS

BY JANE YOLEN

ILLUSTRATED BY JANE DYER

HBJ

HARCOURT BRACE JOVANOVICH, PUBLISHERS

San Diego   New York   London

For Brooke and Cecily

Text copyright © 1987 by Jane Yolen
Illustrations copyright © 1987 by Jane Dyer

Requests for permission to make copies of any
part of the work should be mailed to:
Permissions Department,
Harcourt Brace Jovanovich, Publishers, 8th Floor,
Orlando, Florida 32887.

Library of Congress Cataloging-in-Publication Data
Yolen, Jane.
Piggins.
Summary: During a dinner party, the lights go out
and Mrs. Reynard's beautiful diamond necklace is
stolen, but Piggins the butler quickly discovers the
real thief.
[1. Mystery and detective stories. 2. Pigs —
Fiction] I. Dyer, Jane, ill. II. Title.
PZ7. Y78Pi 1987   [E]   86-22915
ISBN 0-15-261685-3
ISBN 0-15-261686-1 (pbk.)

B C D E F
B C D E (pbk.)

The illustrations in this book were done in colored
pencil and Dr. Martin's watercolors using No. 000
to No. 8 brushes on 140-lb. Fabriano hot press
watercolor paper.
The text type was set in Baskerville No. 2 by
Thompson Type, San Diego, California.
The display type was set in Baskerville by
Thompson Type, San Diego, California.
Color separations were made by Bright Arts
(Hong Kong) Ltd.
Printed and bound by South China Printing Co. Ltd.,
Hong Kong.
Designed by Dalia Hartman
Production supervision by Warren Wallerstein and
Eileen McGlone

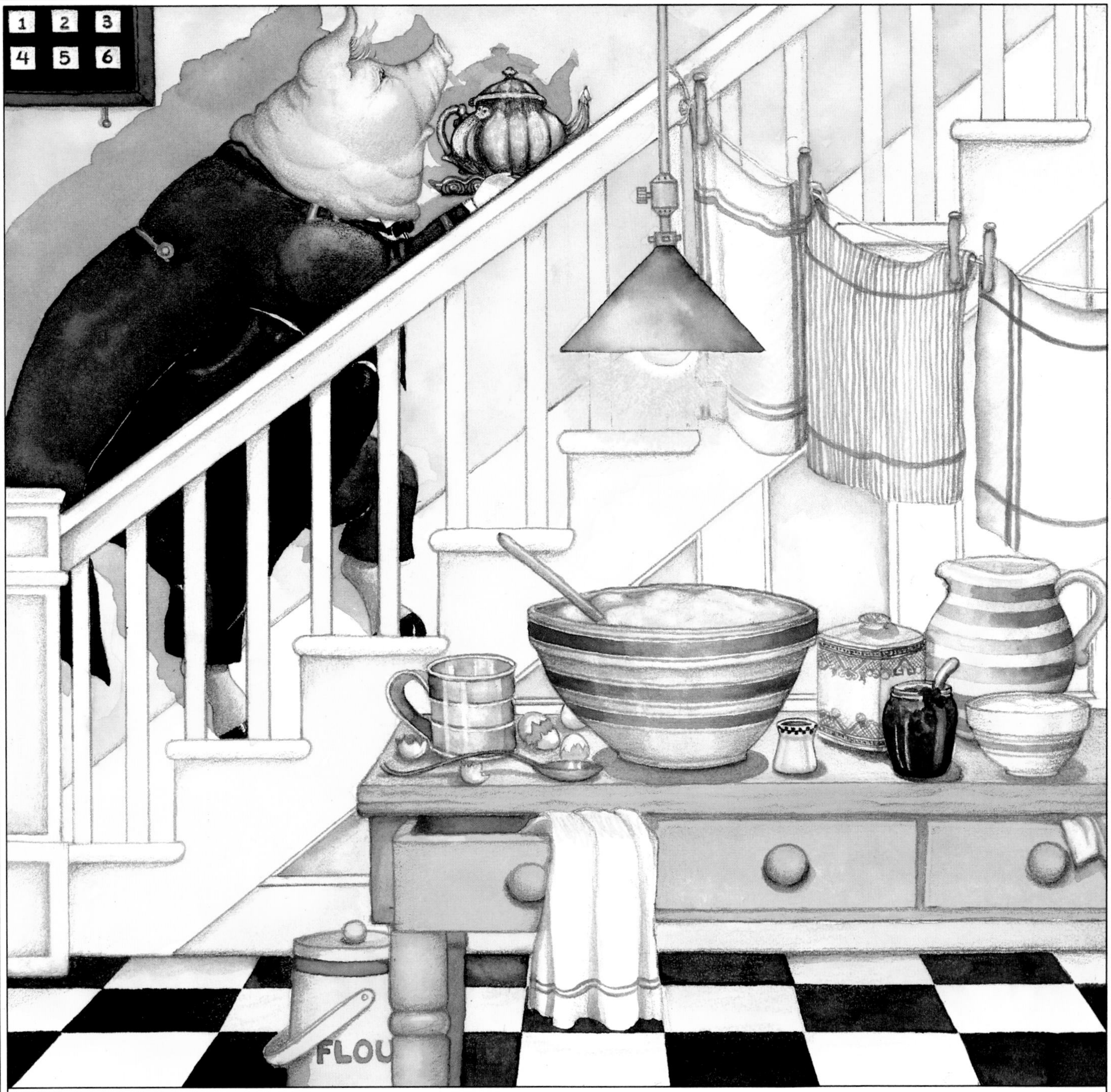
1 2 3
4 5 6
FLOU

Trit-trot, trit-trot. That is the sound of Piggins, the butler at 47 The Meadows, going up the stairs. He has shined the silver teapot so well he can see his snout in it.

UPSTAIRS   Mrs. Reynard is in a terrible dither.

"I cannot find my diamond lavaliere," she says to her husband.

"Is it missing again?" Mr. Reynard asks. "Perhaps one of the servants took it." His whiskers twitch.

"*Our* Cook? *Our* Sara? *Our* Jane? Not possible," says Mrs. Reynard.

Mr. Reynard smiles widely enough so that his teeth show. "Perhaps the butler did it."

"*Our* Piggins?" Mrs. Reynard is clearly shocked. " He *finds* things. He does not *take* things."

"I know, my dear," says Mr. Reynard. "I was making a little joke. Look again and I will help you." He gets up from his chair.

They look and look. At last they find the necklace right where it belongs—in Mrs. Reynard's jewelry box.

BELOW STAIRS   Cook has just removed the cake from the oven. The kitchen is sweet with its smell. Sara, the scullery maid, has scrubbed the pots and pans. She looks as if she needs a scrubbing herself. Upstairs Jane has finished setting the table. Everything is in its proper place.

IN THE DINING ROOM   Piggins is pleased. The glasses sparkle. The silver gleams. Even the chandelier glitters like a thousand diamonds.

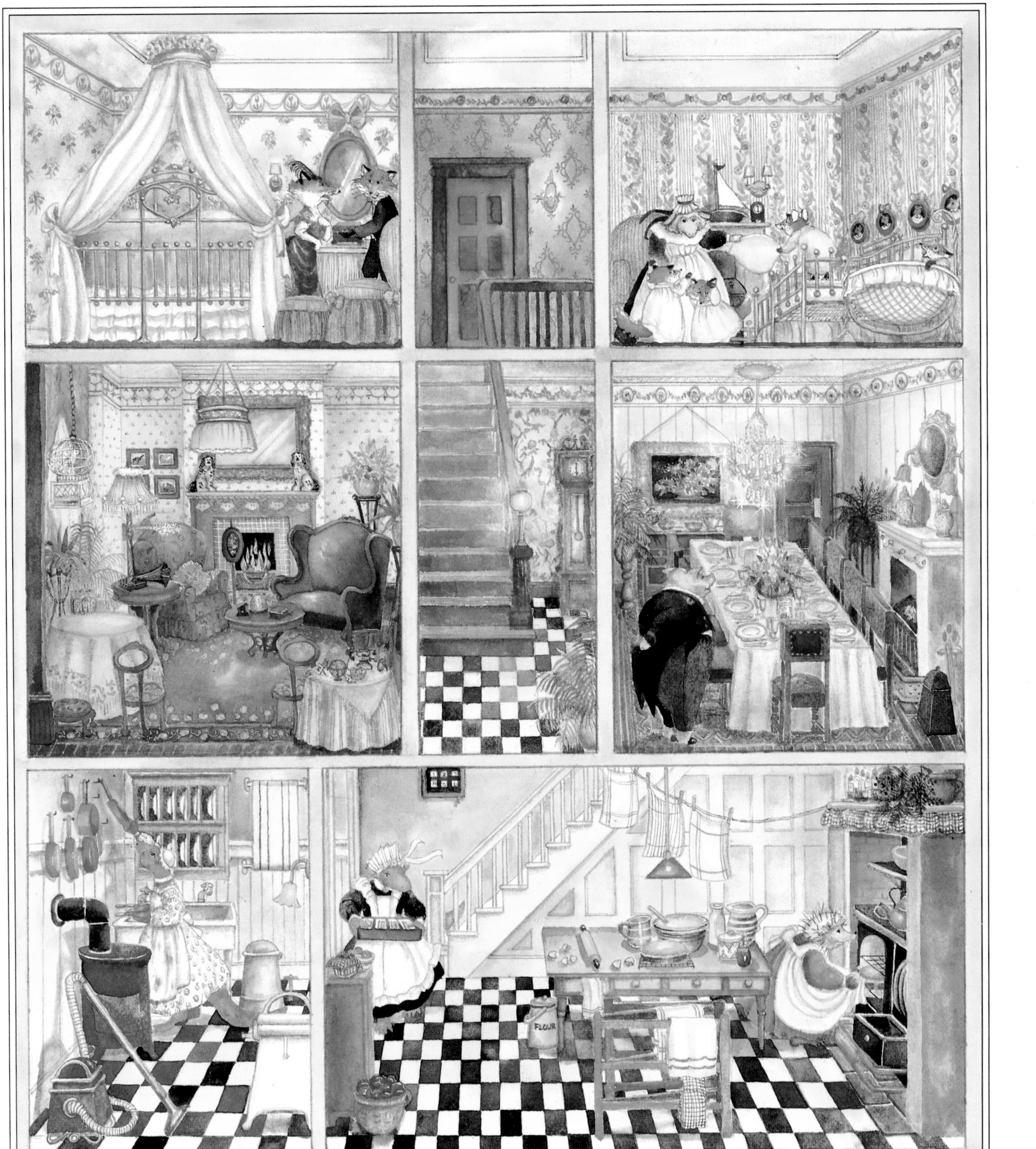
FLOUR

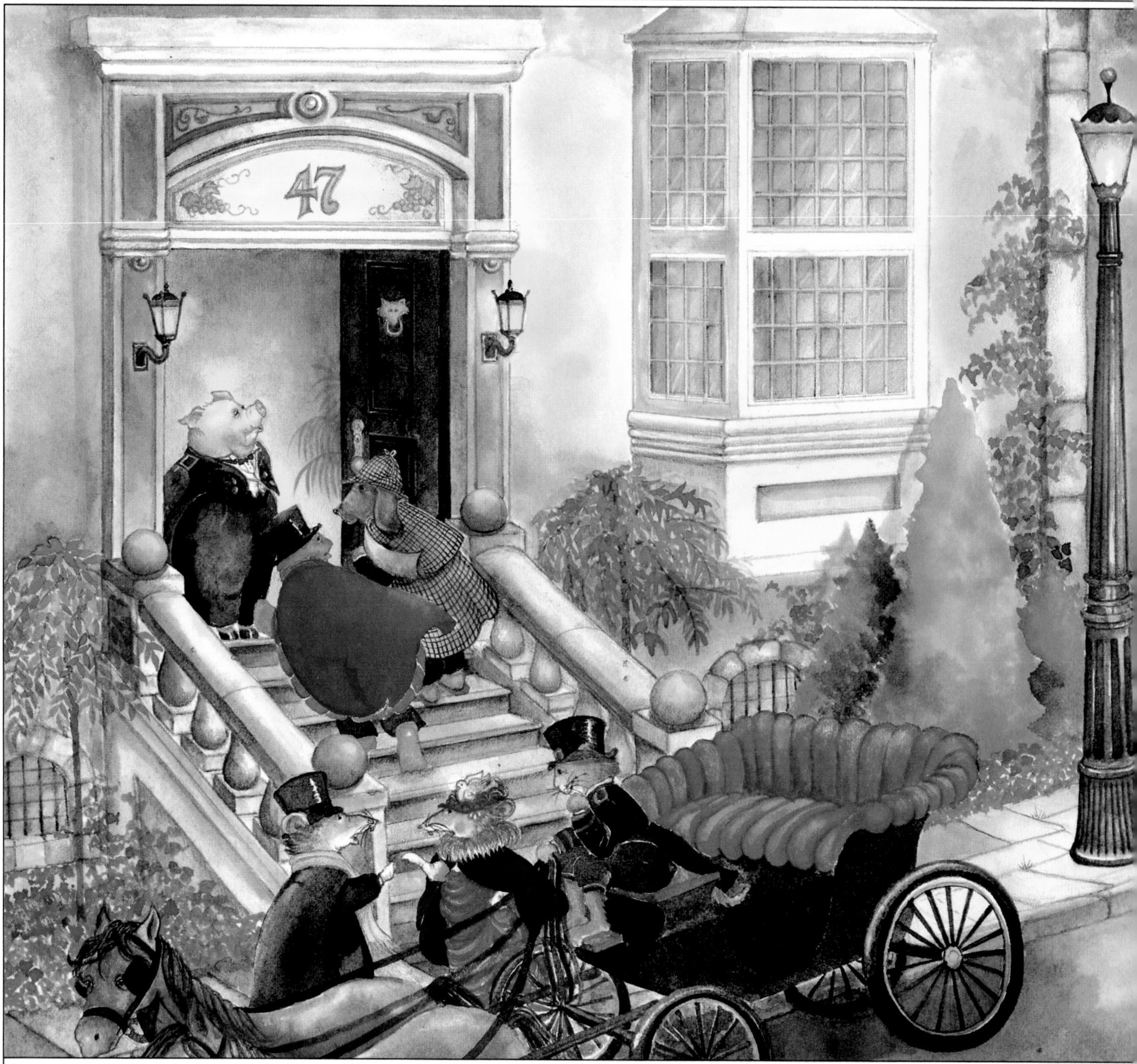
47

Ding-dong. That is the front door bell. Piggins goes to answer it. The dinner guests have started to arrive.

Inspector Bayswater and his friend Professor T. Ortoise are on the steps. The professor is telling a joke. Lord and Lady Ratsby alight

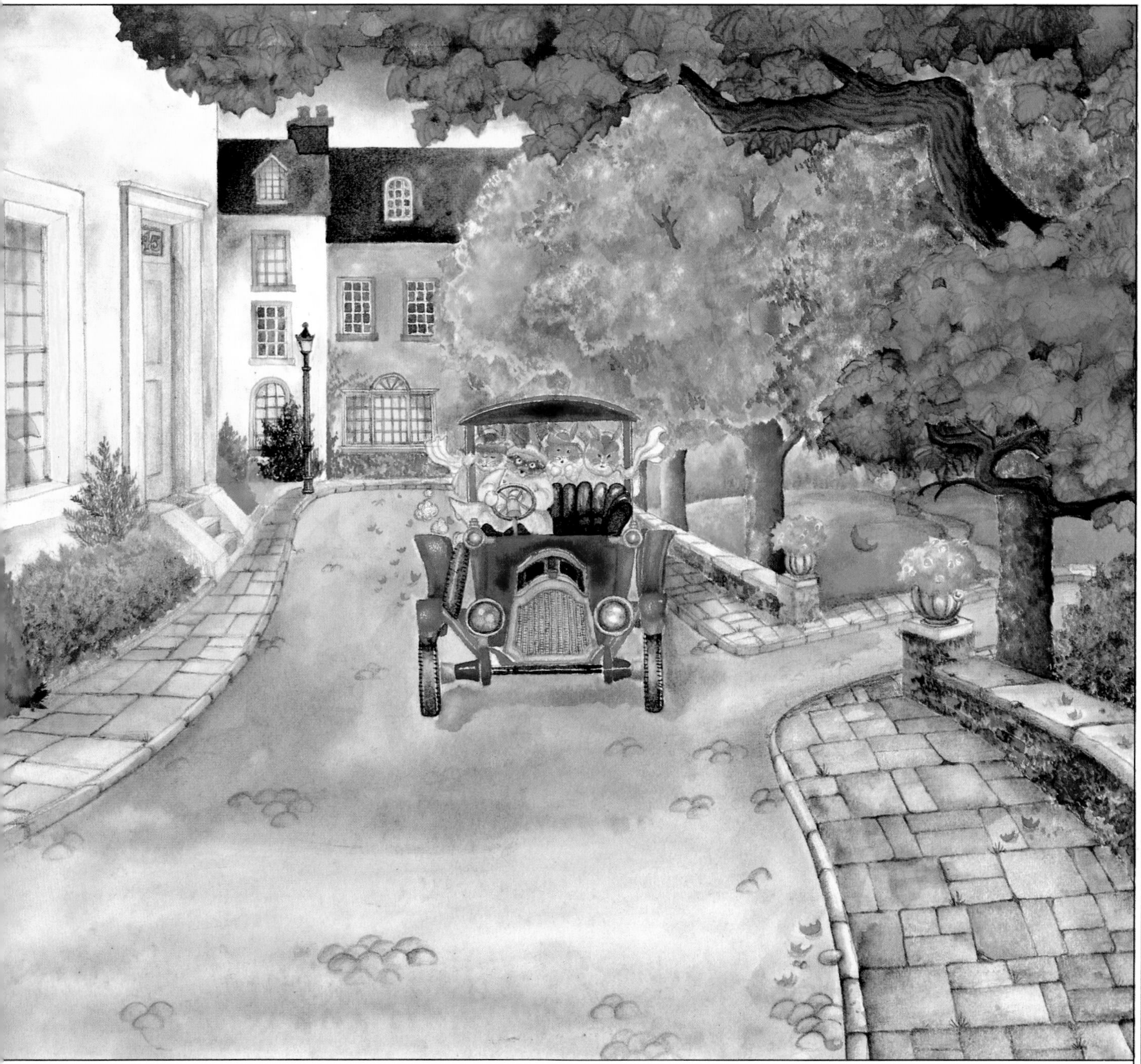

from a carriage. They are arguing with the driver over the fare. Down the street comes the motorcar of the world-famous explorer Pierre Lapin and his three unmarried sisters. He honks the horn. *Aaaa-OOOO-ga. Aaaa-OOOO-ga.* His sisters scream with delight.

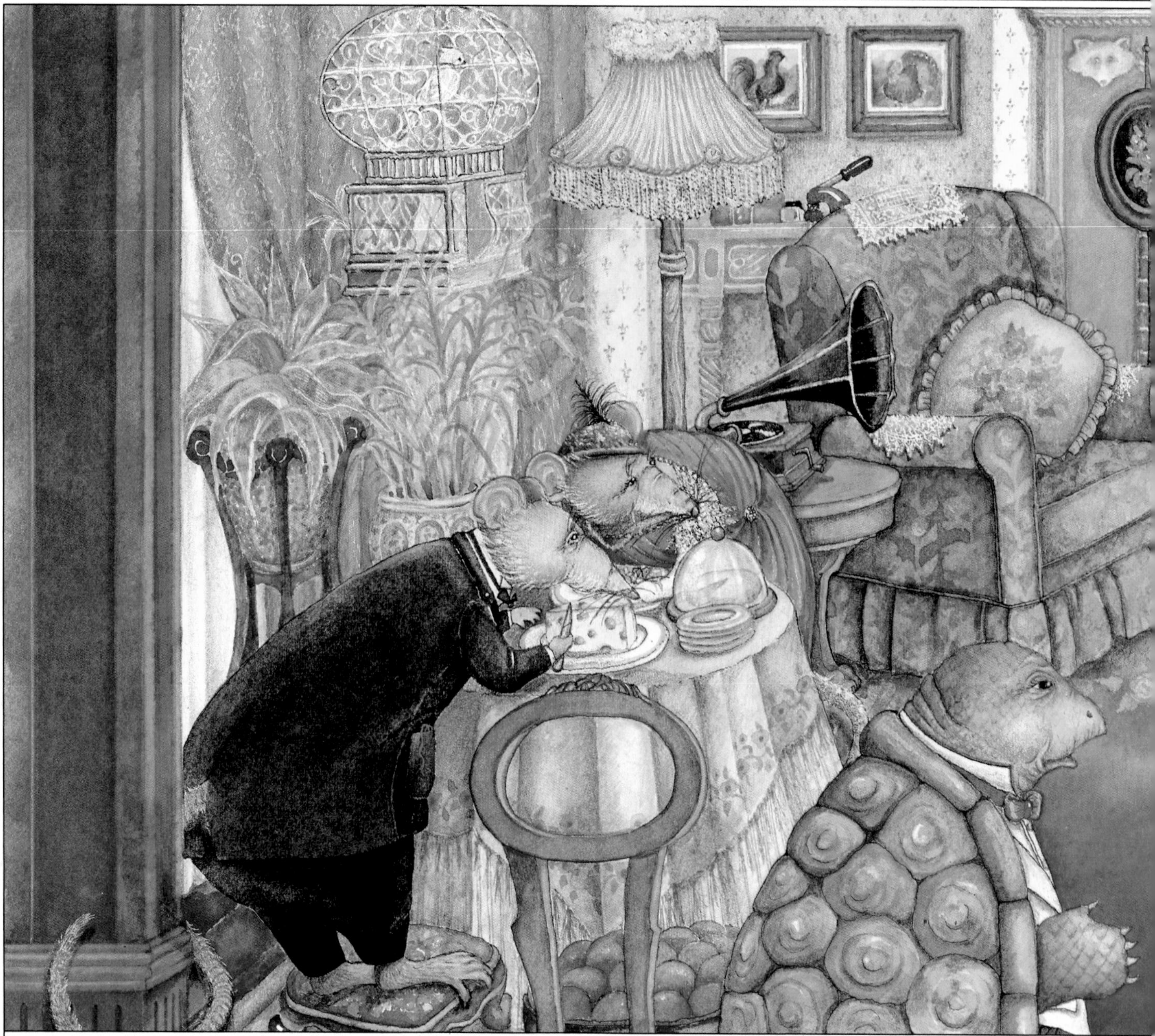

"Lovely weather," says the professor in the living room. He is famous for his conversation. His students all say proudly, "Professor T. Ortoise taught us."

Lord and Lady Ratsby eye the cheeses hungrily. They sample every cheese and even slip a few pieces into their pockets.

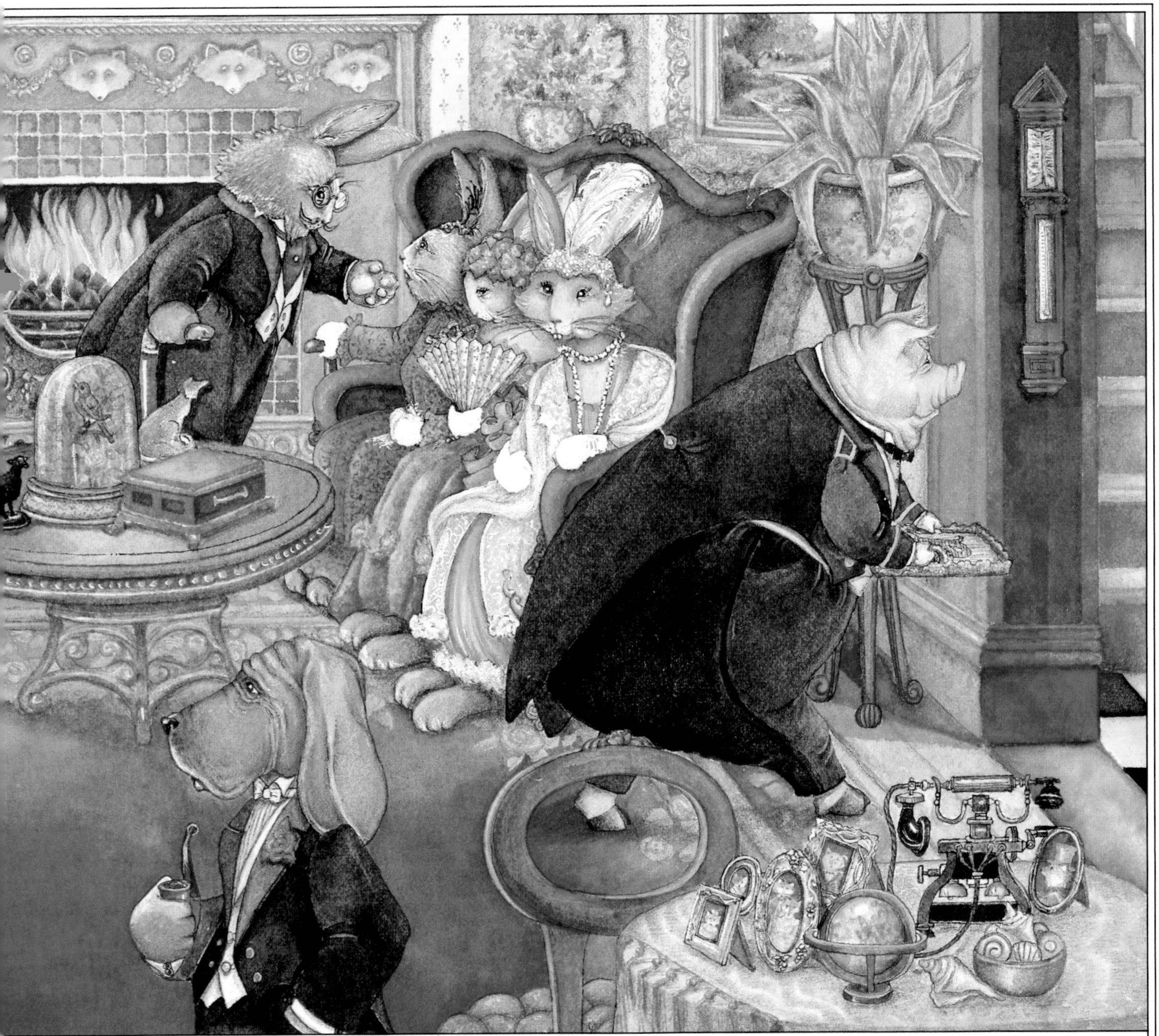

Inspector Bayswater takes out his pipe. He does not light it. The doctors have advised him not to smoke.

Pierre Lapin settles his sisters. "Do you want something to drink?" he asks them.

"Anything but tea," the eldest says. The other two giggle.

Mr. and Mrs. Reynard come into the room and smile warmly at their friends. They greet each of them by name. Everyone admires Mrs. Reynard's diamond lavaliere.

"You may wonder why I have asked you here this evening," says Mr. Reynard.

But no one *really* wonders. Mr. Reynard is a tinkerer. He loves to invite friends over to show off his latest invention.

Mr. Reynard surprises them. "Tonight I will say nothing about my inventions, though I do have one or two small new things." He waves his paw toward several strange contraptions in the corner of the room. "Tonight I want to tell you about—"

"Dinner is served," announces Piggins.

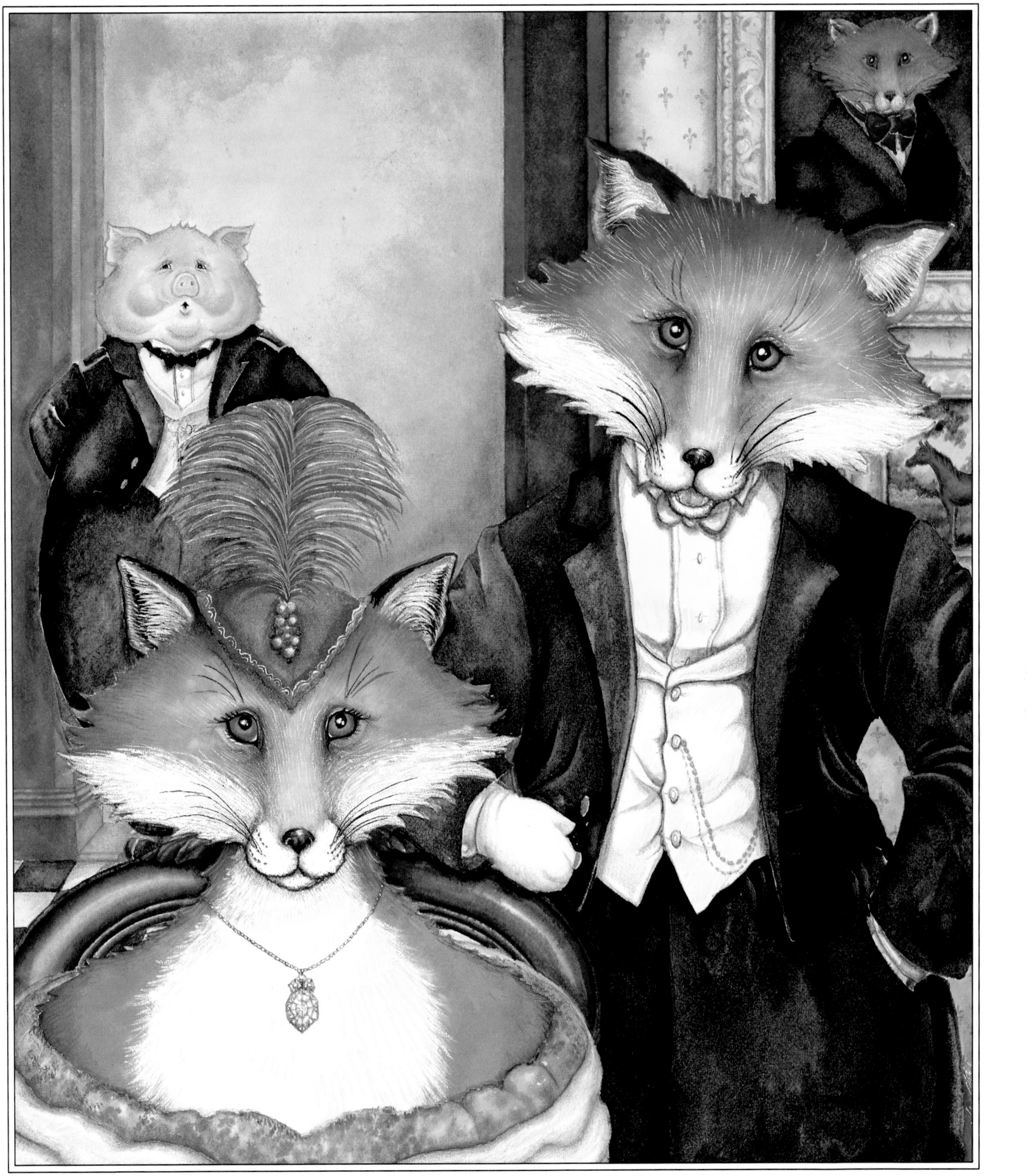

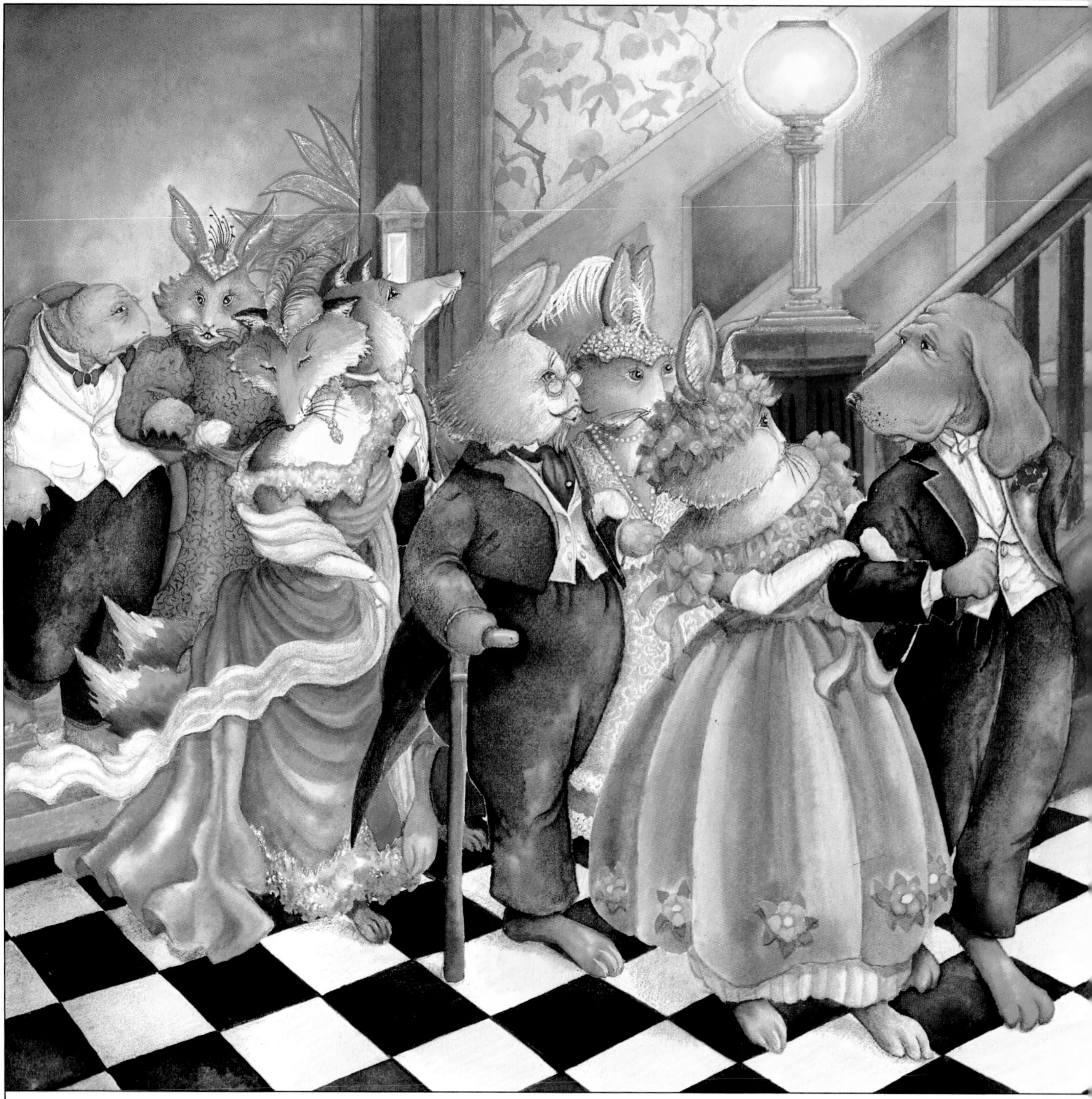

So two by two they go in to dinner. Lord and Lady Ratsby are so hungry they scamper on ahead. Slow but steady, the professor

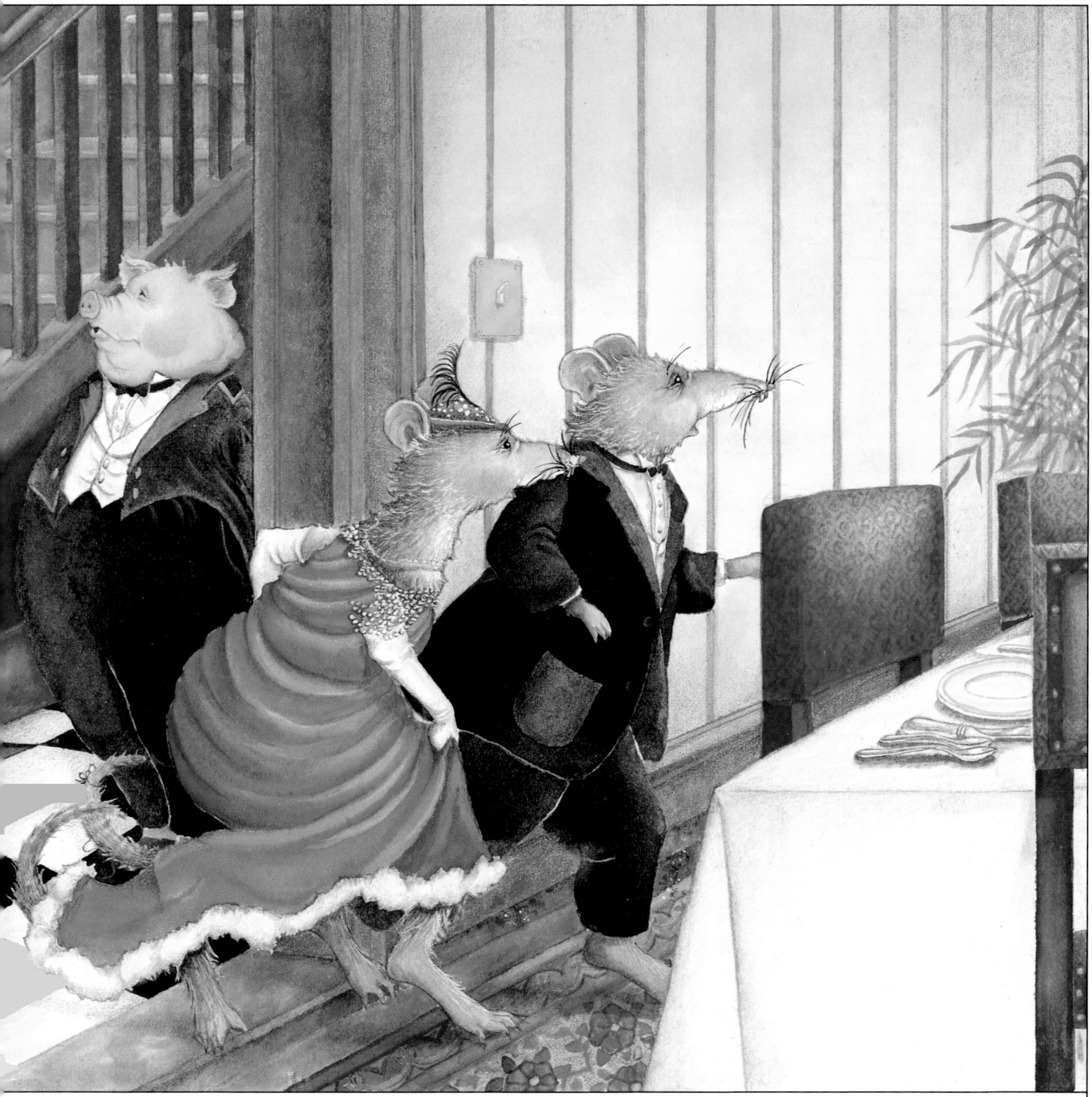

brings up the rear, the eldest Miss Lapin on his arm. It would simply not do to let Cook's wonderful food get cold.

When the shrimp soup has been served, Mr. Reynard smiles. "I have invited you to dinner tonight so that you can admire my wife's brand-new diamond necklace. And so you can hear the story of why we must sell it."

"Sell it?" The eldest Miss Lapin leans forward. "But it is so beautiful. How could you bear to part with it?"

"It must be worth a great deal of money," says Lady Ratsby. She fingers her own necklace, a simple gold chain.

"Yes, it *is* beautiful," says Mrs. Reynard. "And quite expensive. But . . ."

"But what?" asks the inspector. His professional interest has been aroused.

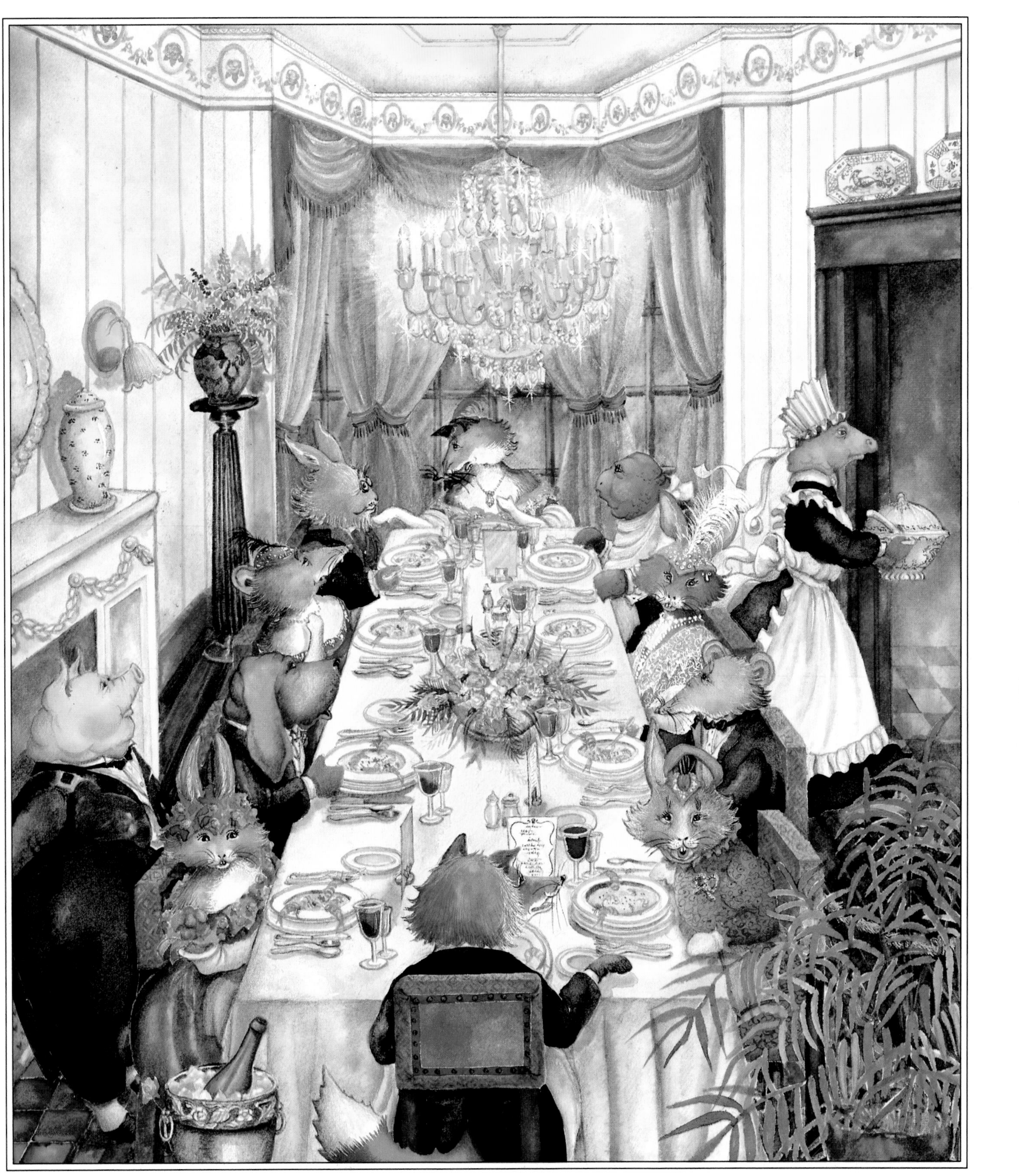

"There is a curse on the diamond!" says Mr. Reynard.

"A curse!" Everyone talks at once.

Mr. Reynard silences them by holding up his right paw. "Yes—a curse! The miner who found the diamond broke his arm. The cutter who shaped it broke all his tools. The store that sold the necklace burned down right after the sale."

"And you?" asks the professor, keeping the conversation going.

"Yes," says Pierre Lapin. "What has happened to you?"

Mrs. Reynard looks sad. "I have lost the lavaliere three times already. Sara broke a bowl and a glass. Cook's first cake flopped. The children have the fox pox. And—"

"Nothing serious has happened . . . yet," says Mr. Reynard. "But just in case, we have decided to sell the lavaliere as soon as possible. I know all of you are interested in gems, so I called you together tonight."

"We are interested indeed," says Lord Ratsby. *"What good timing!"*

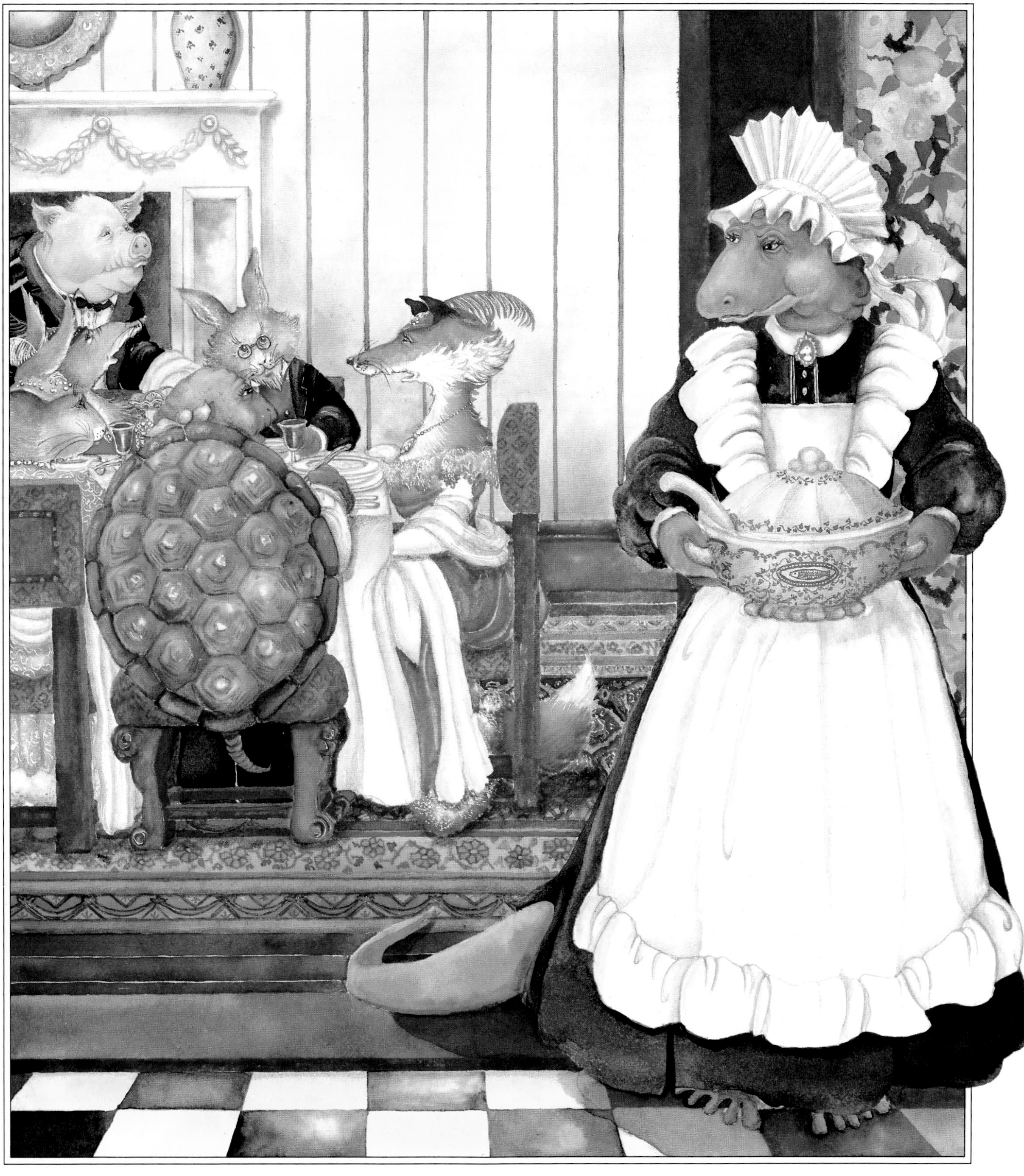

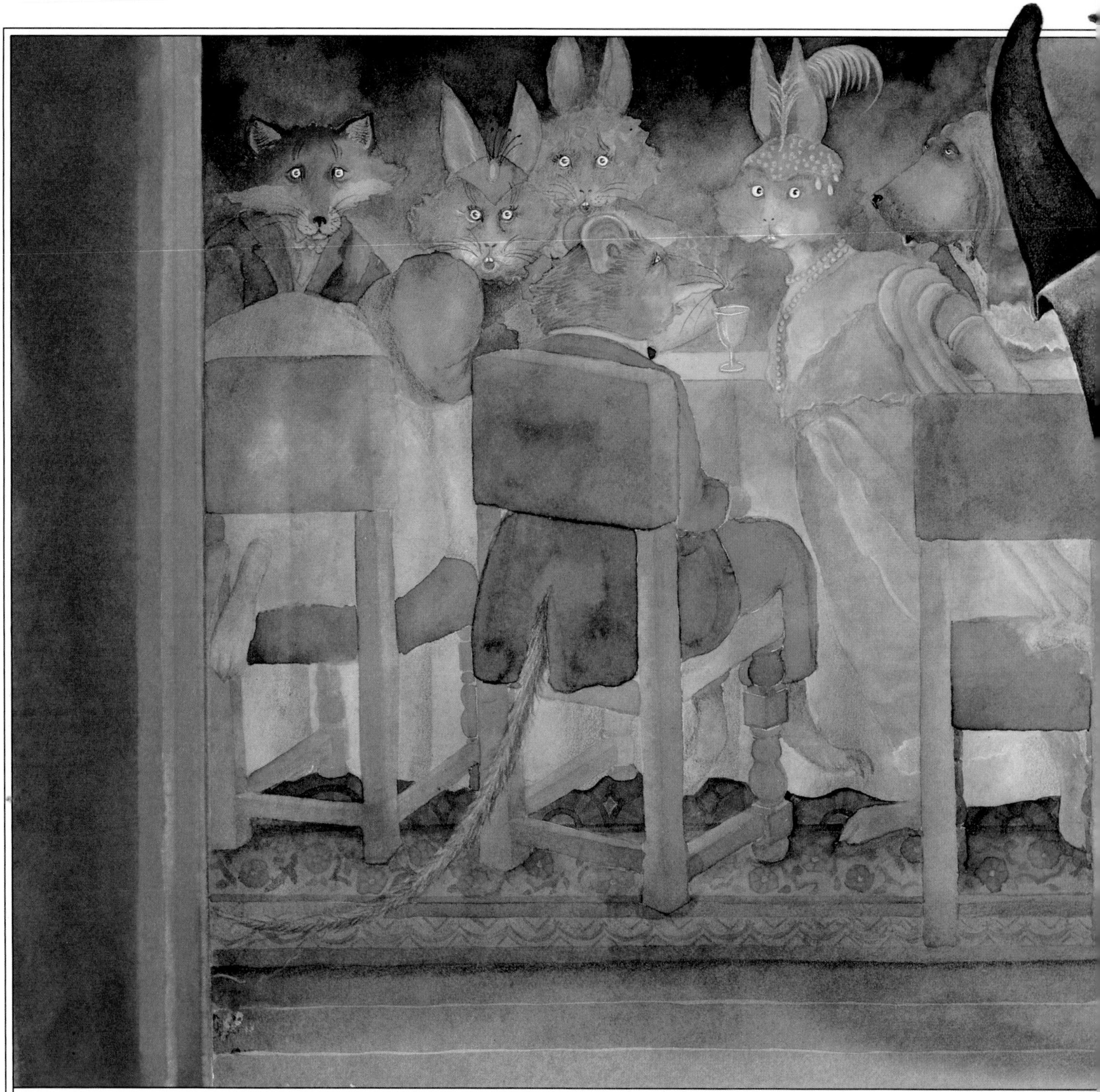

Suddenly the lights go out.
A strange tinkling sound is heard.
There is a scramble of feet.

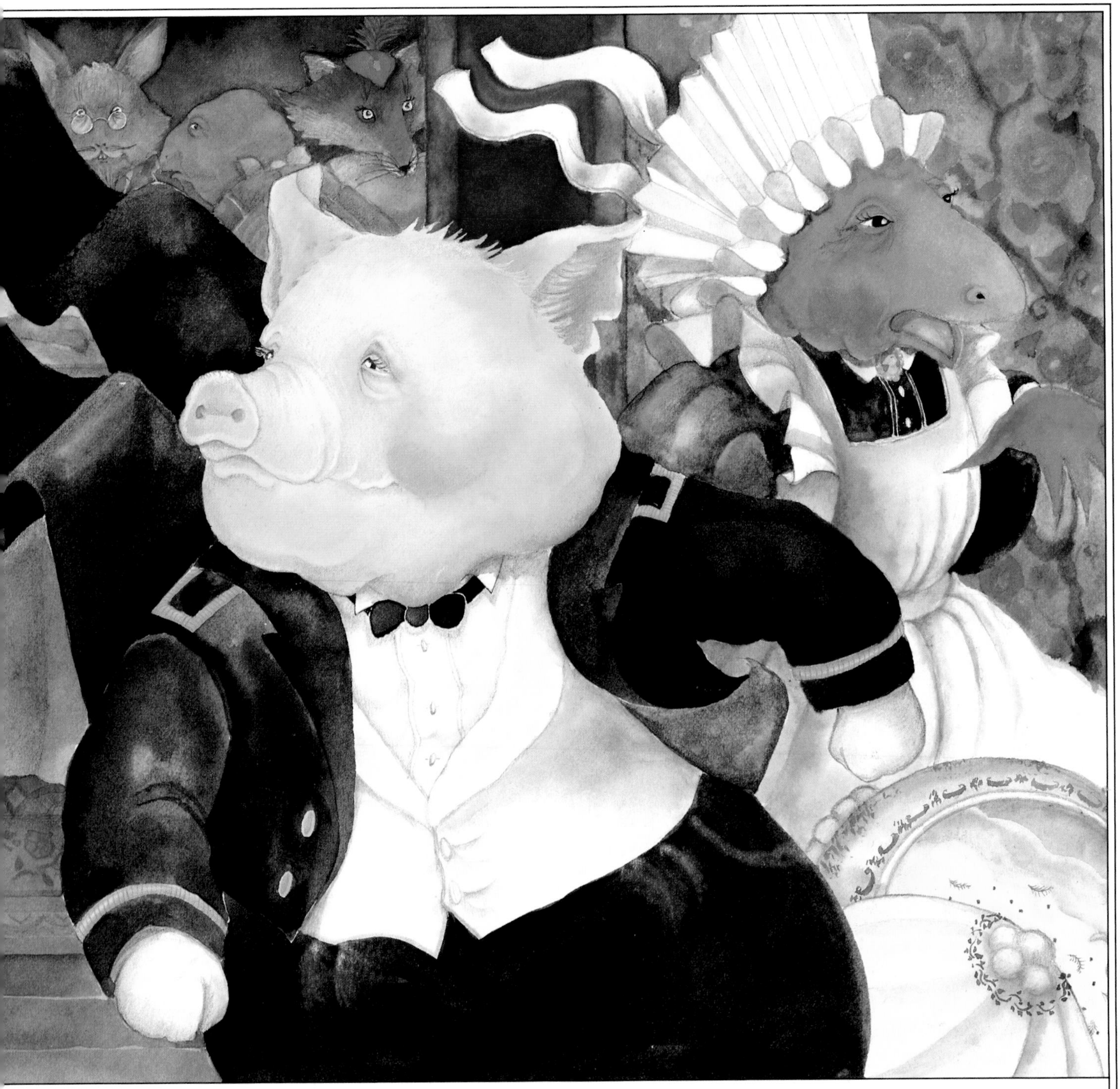

Several objects thud to the floor.
There is a high, squeaky scream.

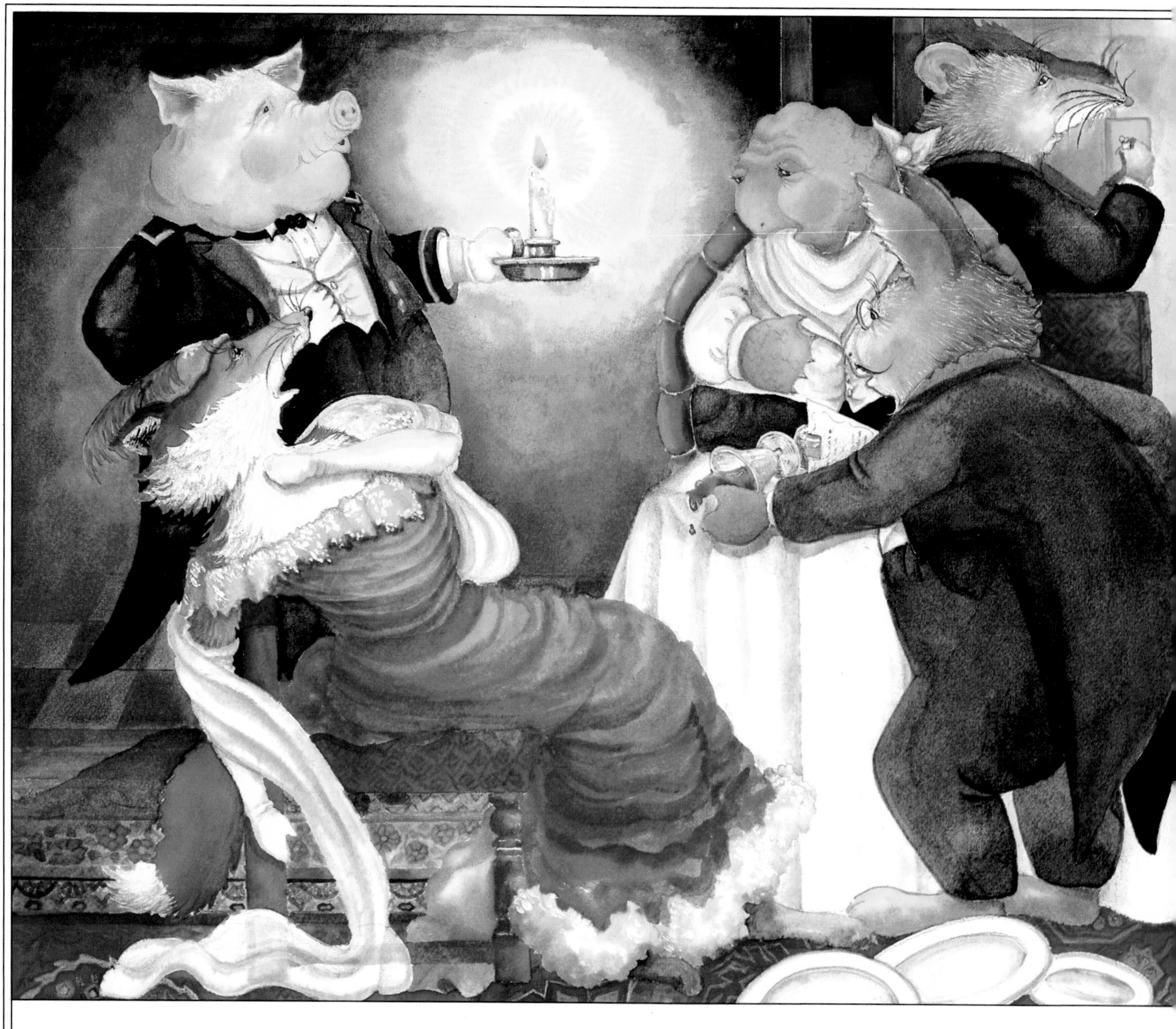

In comes Piggins with a candle.

Lord Ratsby finds the light switch and turns on the glittering chandelier.

Professor T. Ortoise stands up.

Pierre Lapin sets the table aright.

Just then Mrs. Reynard clutches her throat. She screams.

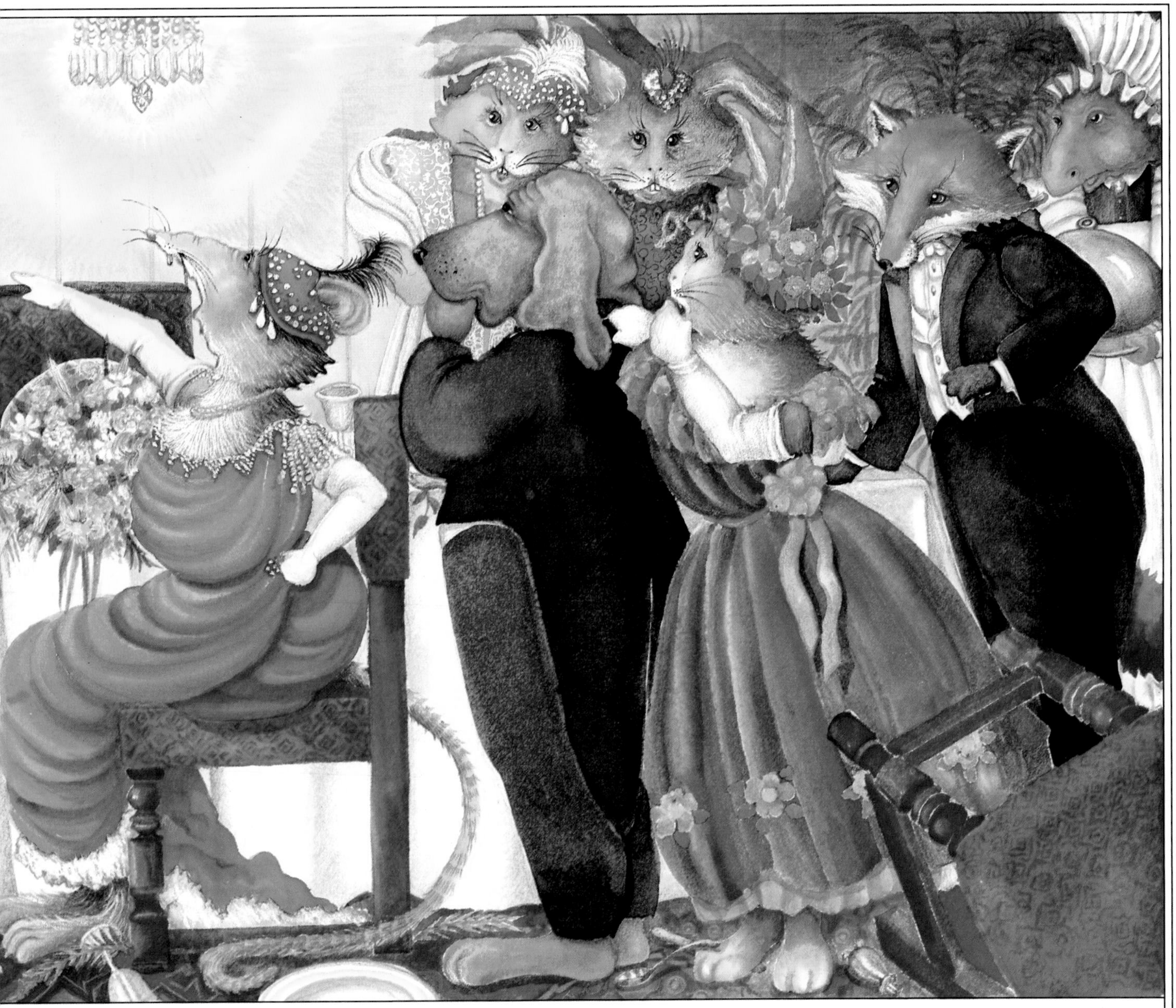

"My diamond lavaliere. It is gone." She falls back in a faint.

Lady Ratsby points her finger at Piggins. "Perhaps the butler did it."

"Balderdash and poppycock," says Mr. Reynard. He turns to the inspector. "I cannot believe *our* Piggins did it. Can you find any clues to the real thief?"

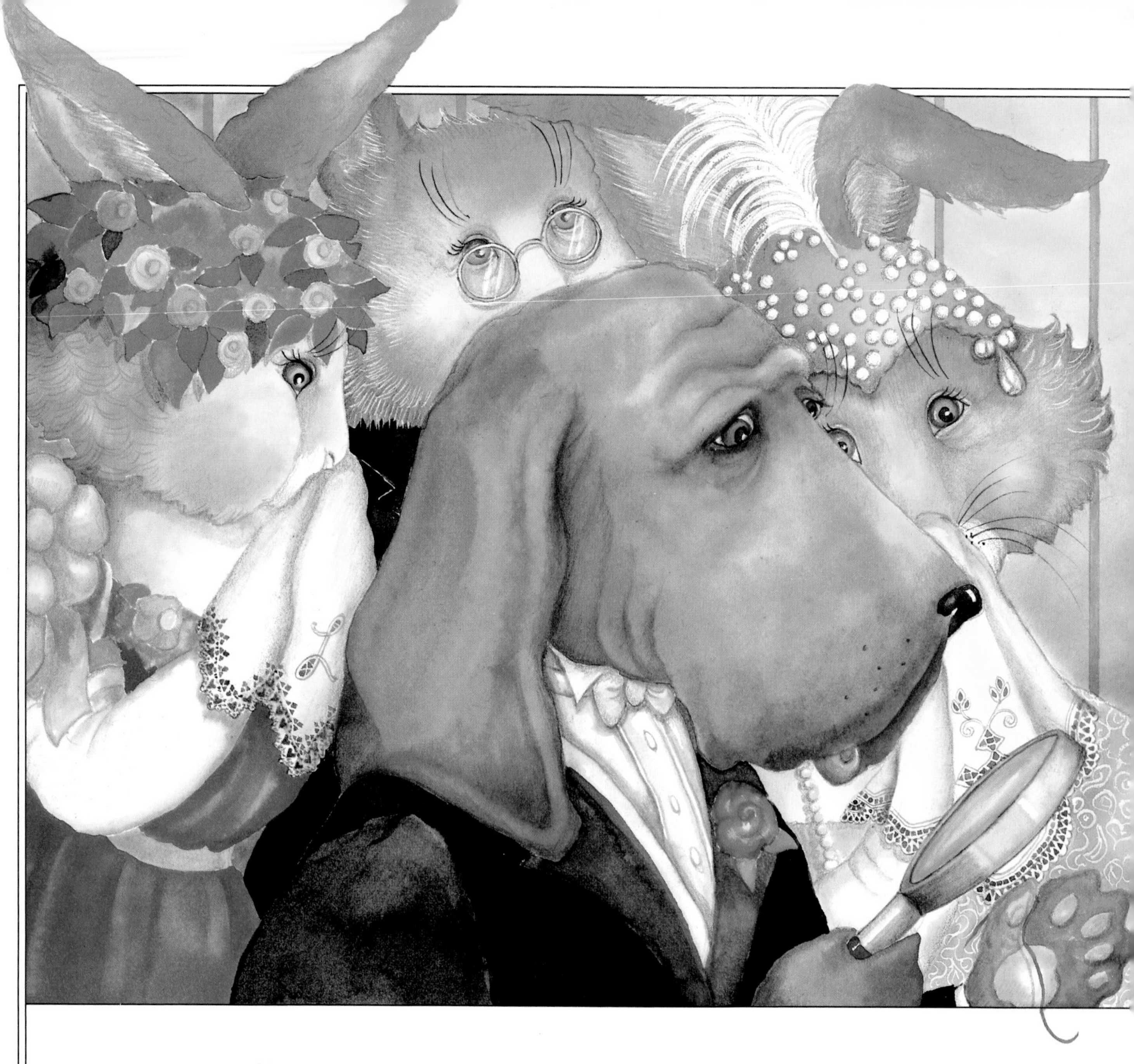

The inspector examines the room. He searches everywhere. He finds a red thread near the door, crumbs on the table, and a little bit of dirt on the floor. He cannot find the diamond lavaliere.

"I am stumped," he says at last.

"Hummmmph!" snorts Lady Ratsby.

Professor T. Ortoise is at a loss for words for the first time in his life.

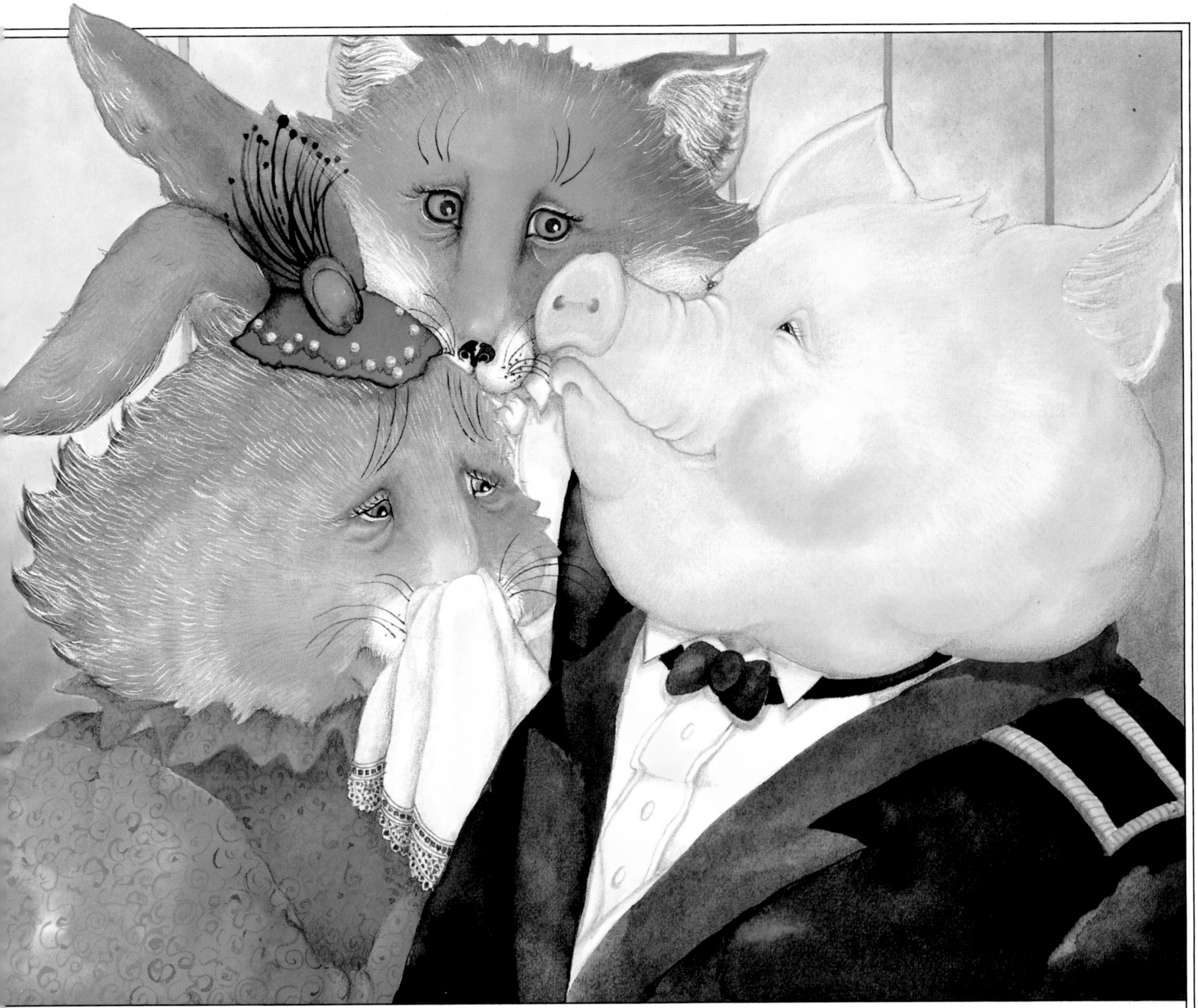

Pierre Lapin comforts his three sisters, who sniffle into their lace handkerchiefs.

Mrs. Reynard comes out of her faint.

Piggins smiles. "I, on the other hand, am not stumped. I know who has done it."

"Good show, Piggins," says Mr. Reynard. "Tell us everything. And I will record it with my latest invention."

"First there are the clues," says Piggins. "A piece of red thread near the door. A trail of cheese crumbs on the table. The tinkling sound we all heard. The scream."

"And the dirt on the floor?" asks the inspector.

"For that I shall have to speak sharply to Upstairs Jane," says Piggins, frowning. "There should be *no* dirt in this house."

"I do not understand the clues," says the professor. "Thread, crumbs, a tinkling sound, a scream."

"There is not one thief—but two," explains Piggins. "One to turn off the lights and make a commotion, and one to steal the diamond lavaliere."

"Oh," says Pierre Lapin. "I know all about making commotions. In my youth, I stole into a farmer's garden and made much too much noise."

"The clues," remind the Misses Lapin together.

Piggins continues. "Before everyone came into dinner, someone tied the red thread to the light switch. At a signal, the thread was pulled and the lights turned off. But the thread was pulled so hard, it broke. In the dark someone grabbed the necklace and stepped up onto the table, leaving a trail of cheese crumbs where no cheese had been served. The tinkling sound was the chandelier being disturbed. The scream was the signal that all was clear."

"Then that means . . ." says Inspector Bayswater.

"That the thieves are . . ." says the professor.

"None other than . . ." says Mr. Reynard.

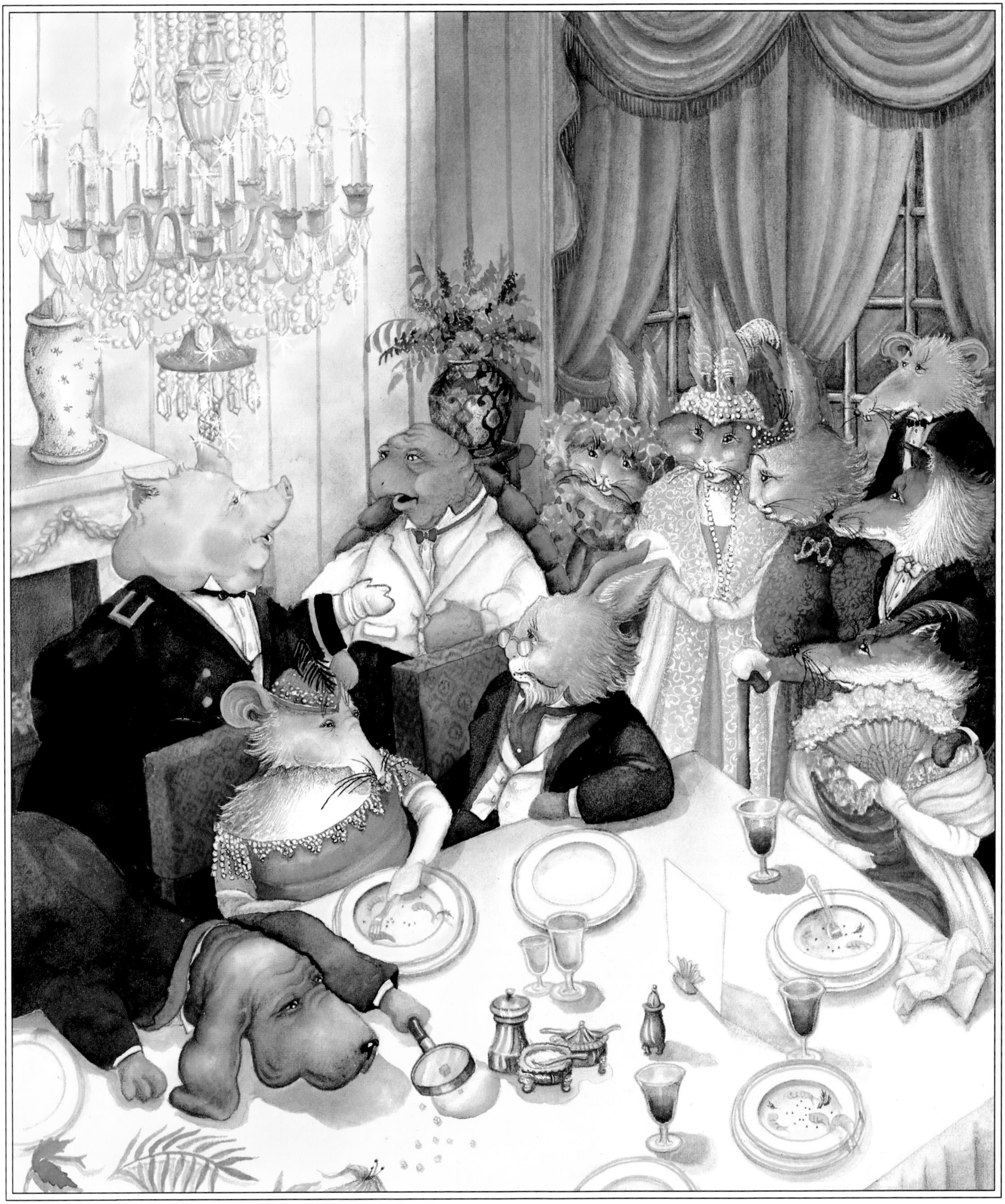

"Lord and Lady Ratsby," finishes Piggins. "They knew about the diamond all along and planned to steal it at their very first chance."

"But where *is* the diamond?" asks the professor. "Inspector Bayswater looked everywhere."

"Yes," sneers Lord Ratsby. "Where is your precious diamond?"

Piggins smiles. "In plain sight." He steps on one of the chairs and reaches up into the glittering chandelier. He finds the necklace.

"I suspected the Ratsbys were broke," says the eldest Miss Lapin. "Lady Ratsby is wearing a simple gold chain. Usually she drips jewels."

"Catch them!" Mrs. Reynard cries, for the Ratsbys are trying to escape.

The eldest Miss Lapin sticks out her foot. She trips Lord Ratsby. The younger Misses Lapin jump on top of Lady Ratsby.

"Well done, Piggins," says Mr. Reynard.

"Well done, girls!" cries Mrs. Reynard.

"Curses!" says Lord Ratsby.

Professor T. Ortoise laughs. "Curses indeed! Perhaps, Reynard, the curse on your lavaliere is at its end."

The police are summoned and they take the Ratsbys away.

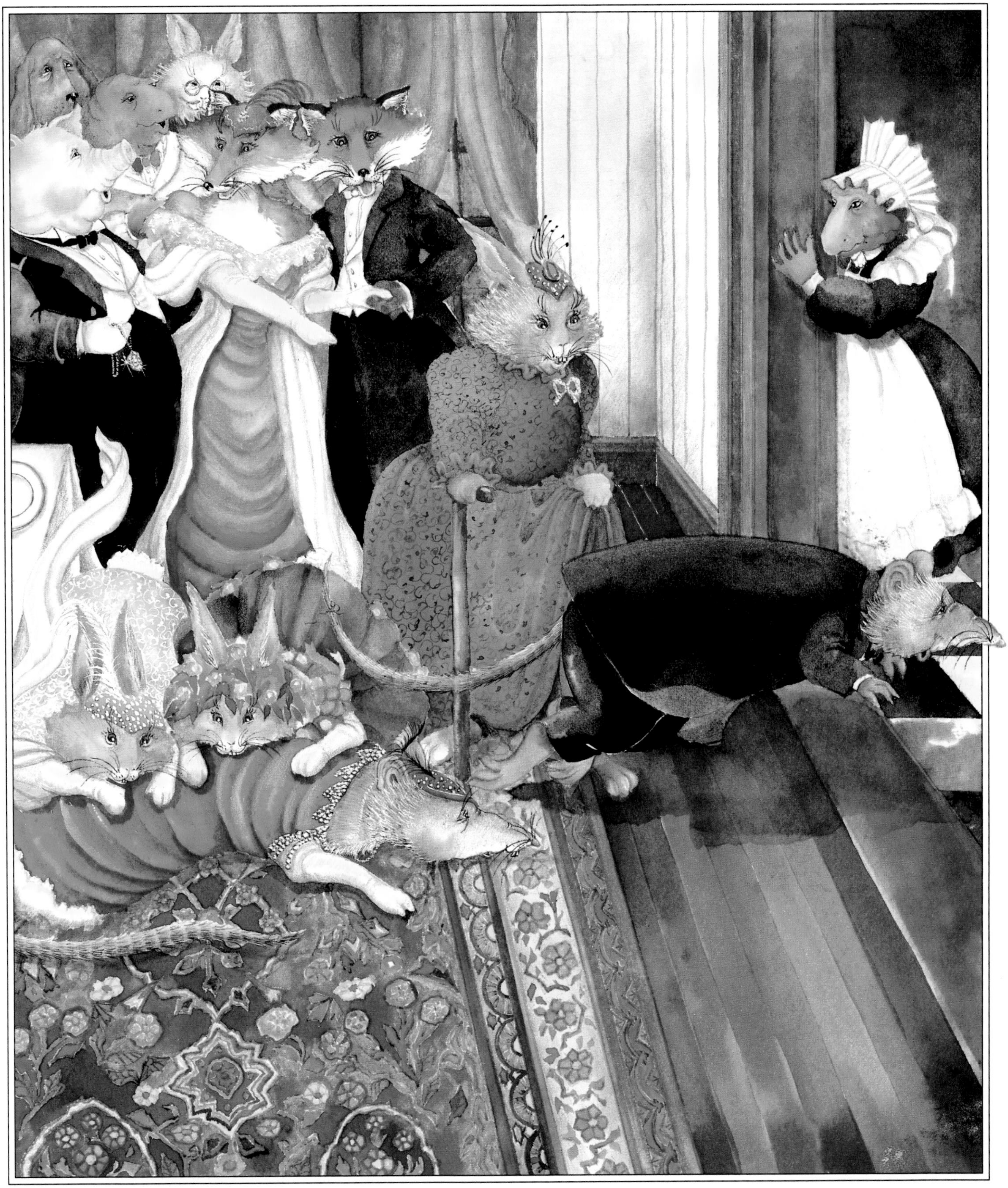

UPSTAIRS   Mr. and Mrs. Reynard get ready for bed. Mrs. Reynard carefully wraps the diamond lavaliere in a velvet cloth. She puts it away in her jewelry box. "I hope the curse *is* ended," she says. "I would hate to part with my beautiful necklace."

Mr. Reynard nods and takes off his tie. "I knew the butler did not do it," he says.

"Not *our* Piggins," says Mrs. Reynard.

BELOW STAIRS   Sara has cleaned the last of the dishes. She could do with a good cleaning herself. Cook snoozes in her chair. And Jane, having swept up the dirt on the dining room floor, has set the kettle on the stove for one last cup of tea.

IN THE DINING ROOM   Everything is quiet and clean. Piggins locks the front door at 47 The Meadows. He hears the kettle whistling.

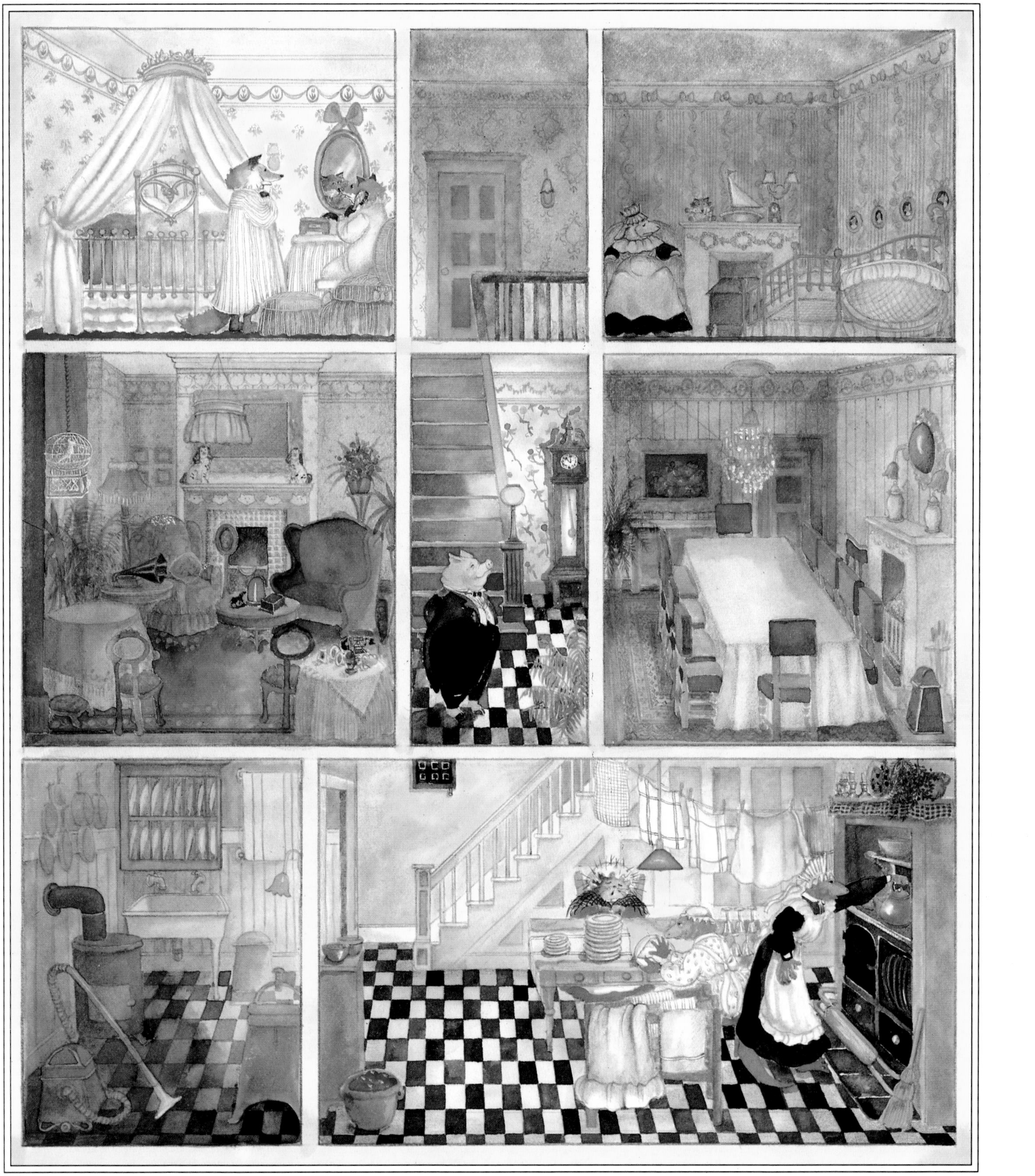

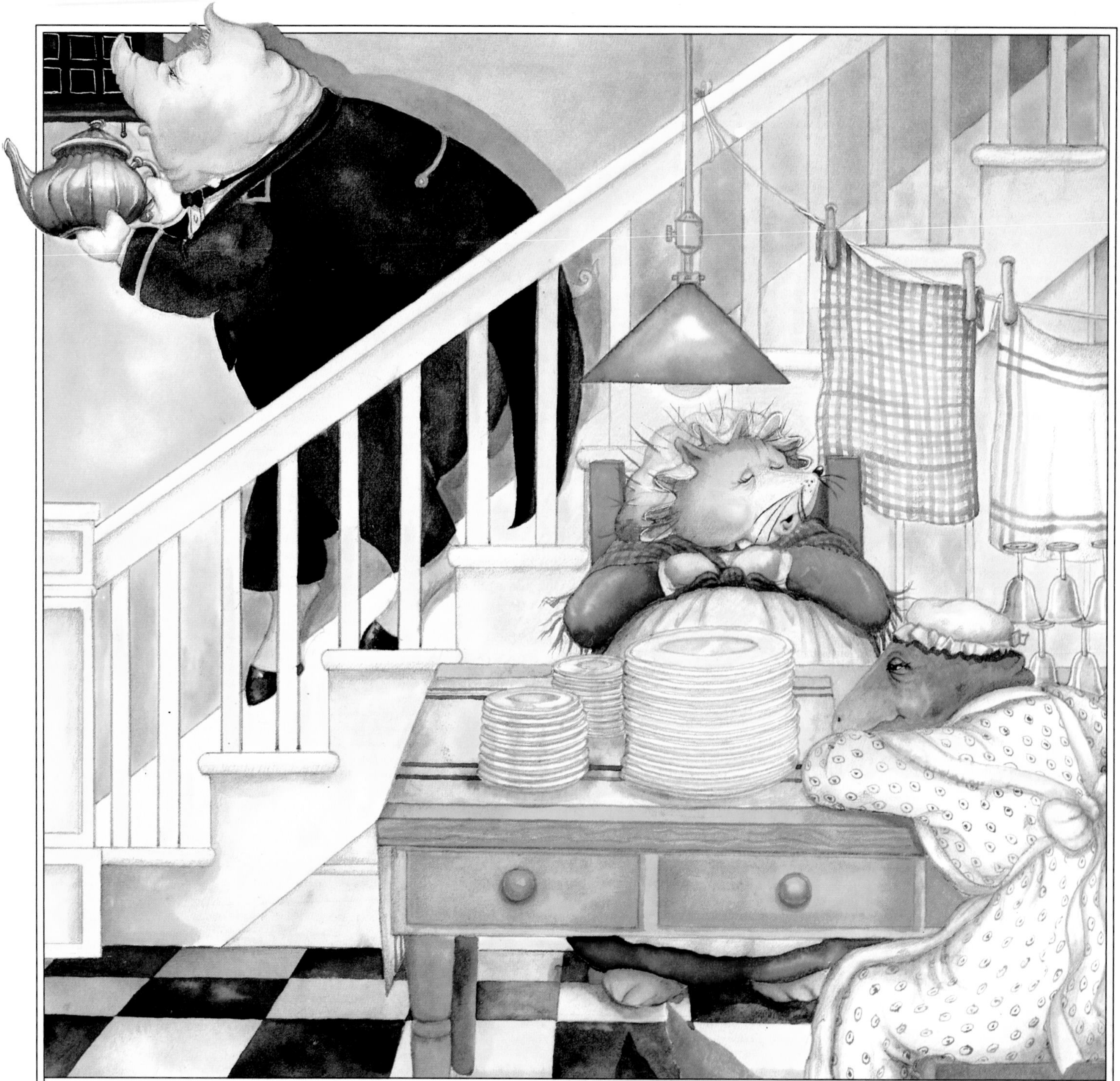

It has been a long and interesting evening. Piggins is tired. Teapot in hand, he goes back down the stairs. *Trit-trot, trit-trot, trit-trot.*